To the biggest little lawn mower fan I know.

Published by LHC Publishing 2016

The Little Mower That Could
Text Copyright © 2016 Yvonne Jones
Illustration Copyright © 2016 Yvonne Jones

All inquiries should be directed to
www.LHCpublishing.com

ISBN-13: 978-0-9970254-4-6
ISBN-10: 0997025441

PUBLISHING

THE LITTLE MOWER THAT COULD

WRITTEN & ILLUSTRATED BY
YVONNE JONES

Krrrr, krrrr, krrrr. Whirr, whirr, whirr. Squeak, squeak, squeak. The heavy garage door rumbled open. It was a cheerful and beautiful day. Bright sunlight fell into the otherwise sparsely lit area. The space was filled with all sorts of interesting things.

4

There were all kinds of machinery - a heavy riding mower, an old-fashioned reel mower, a very blue push mower, and a very, very quiet electric mower. And there was other equipment as well - a trusty leaf blower, a powerful weed trimmer, an old and rusty shovel, a handy rake, a pair of very sharp hedge shears, and every kind of equipment needed to keep a yard tidy and neat.

But that was not all. In the very corner of the garage stood a big timber box filled to the brim with all sorts of toys for little boys and girls - a wooden car, a colorful train, a wide-eyed doll, a yellow rubber duck, and a cheerfully dotted bouncy ball.

Recent weather had brought lots of rain, which had made the grass grow and grow, and become lush and thick. Birds were singing, insects were buzzing, and air conditioners were humming. But what a commotion there was coming from the toy box standing in the corner! All the toys just loved to play in the blooming grassy area in the warm afternoon sun. So off they dashed - the wooden car zoomed down the driveway, the colorful train rolled between the hedges, the wide-eyed doll gazed at the blue summer's sky, the yellow rubber duck waddled along the path, and the cheerfully dotted bouncy ball bounced toward the grass. Then all of a sudden a little cry rang through the air.

"Help! Help! I'm stuck! I'm stuck!" the little voice sniveled. It was the cheerfully dotted bouncy ball. She was stuck in the high and thick grass. She tried and she tried, but she could not roll another inch.

How were the other toys going to help the bouncy ball get out of the tall grass?

"Let's ask the heavy riding mower," said the wooden car that came rolling back up the driveway. "Maybe he can help us cut a path."

So together, the toys cried out loud: "Please, mighty and heavy riding mower, can you please help us mow a path to our friend, the cheerfully dotted bouncy ball? She is stuck in the tall grass and can't move an inch. We won't be able to get to her unless you help us."

But the mighty and heavy riding mower let out an ear-splitting rumble:
"GRRRAKKA KKAKKAKKAKKAKKAKKAKK!
You want me to help you? I am a heavy-duty garden tool with the most powerful engine there is. I have cut more grass than you've ever seen. I have an attachable collection box and can drive in circles. Waste my valuable gas on toys like you? I think not!" And off he rumbled to the other side of the garage.

How sad the little ball and all the other toys felt!

Then the colorful train called out, "The heavy riding mower is not the only one in the world. There is another mower. His blades look razor-sharp and in good shape. Let's ask him to help us."

The colorful train blew his whistle and steered out from under the hedges.

"Please, whirly hand-reel mower," cried all the toys together. "Can you please help us mow a path to our friend, the cheerfully dotted bouncy ball? She is stuck in the tall grass and can't move an inch. We won't be able to get to her unless you help us."

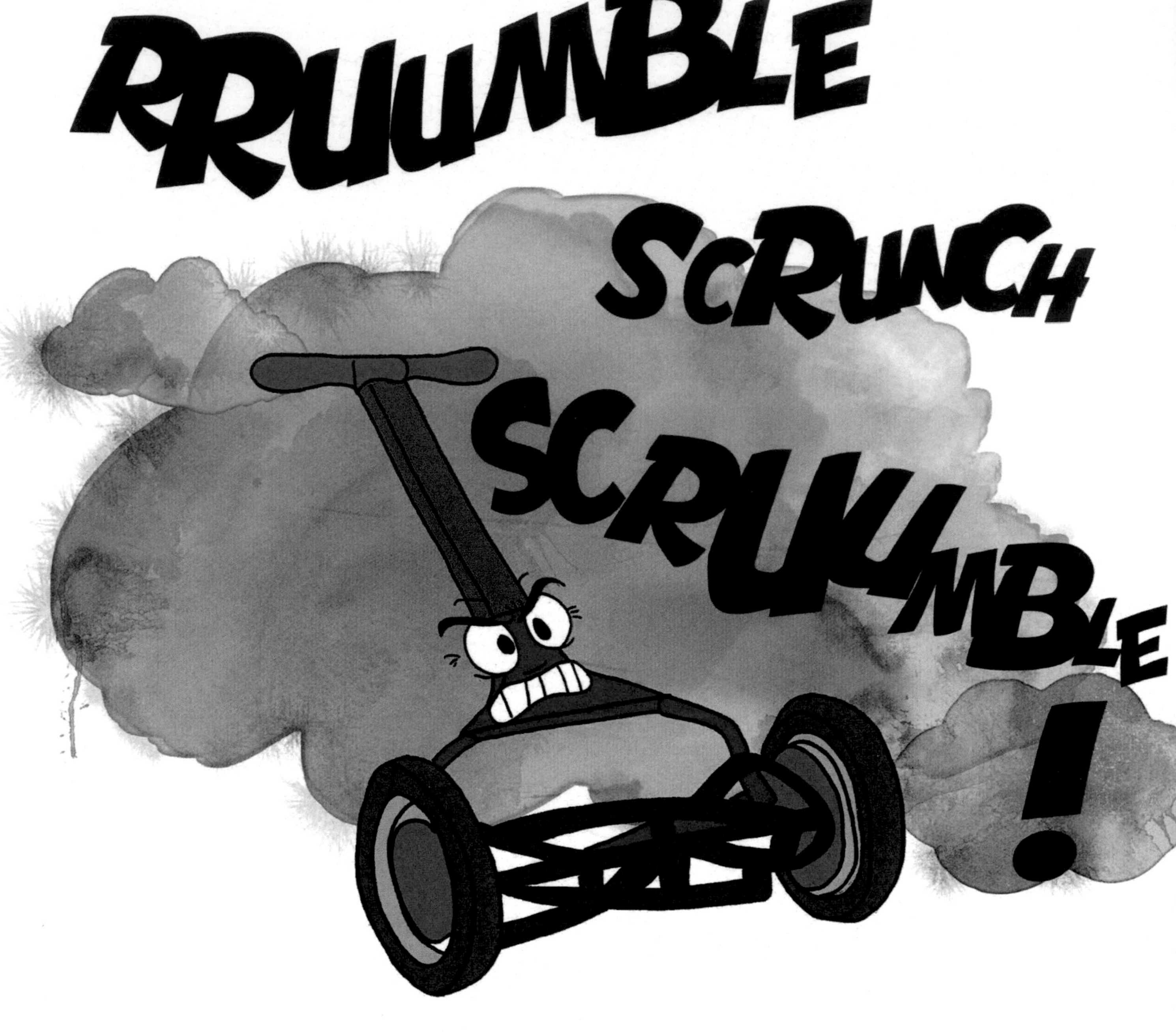
RRUUMBLE
SCRUNCH
SCRUUMBLE
!

But the whirly hand reel mower rattled out loud: **"RRUUMBLE SCRUNCH SCRUUMBLE SCRUUUNCHH!** I am a lightweight and height-adjustable reel lawn mower. My cutting cylinder slices through blades of grass like a pair of scissors. My large wheels have a special tread pattern that lets me move easily, even on thick grass. I am a very important mower. I won't help toys like you!" And the whirly hand reel mower wheeled himself angrily toward his corner of the garage.

The little ball and all other toys were very sad.

"Don't worry," exclaimed the wide-eyed doll. "The whirly hand reel mower is not the only one in the world. There is another mower. He looks very powerful and sturdy. Let's ask him to help us."

So the pretty wide-eyed doll toddled out of the sun toward the powerful and sturdy push mower.

"Please, very blue push mower," cried all the toys together. "Can you please help us mow a path to our friend, the cheerfully dotted bouncy ball? She is stuck in the tall grass and can't move an inch. We won't be able to get to her unless you help us."

But the very blue push mower droned:
"PPPPPPPP PPPPPPPP PPPPPPP!
I am the sturdiest and loudest push model available. I am very fierce. I have a pull cord to start my engine. And I guzzle down expensive gasoline like no other. My starter rope is brand new and I will not wear it out just to help toys like you. I will not." And off he rumbled toward the other mowers.

Then indeed the little ball was very, very sad, and the other toys were ready to cry.

But the yellow rubber duck called out, "Here is another mower, a bright green one. He's very quiet, but maybe he will help us."

The very quiet electric mower slowly wheeled out of the shadows of the garage and into the sun. When he saw all the worried toys, he asked kindly, "What's the matter, my friends?"

"Oh, whispering electric mower," cried all the toys together. "Can you please help us mow a path to our friend, the cheerfully dotted bouncy ball? She is stuck in the tall grass and can't move an inch. We won't be able to get to her unless you help us."

"I am not the toughest model," said the whispering green electric mower. "I am battery-powered and have a push button for an easy start, but they don't use me often. Never before have I cut grass this thick and high."

"But we must get to the cheerfully dotted bouncy ball before nightfall, so she won't have to spend all night alone in the yard," said all the toys.

The whispering green electric mower looked up and saw the tears in the toys' eyes. And he thought of the poor little ball that would have to spend the night in the yard all alone unless he helped.

Then the whispering green electric mower said, "I know I can do it. I know I can do it. I know I can do it." And he pressed his start button with a firm push. The engine briefly chortled, and then began to whirr.

"**RIZZZZZ RIZZZZZ RIZZZZZ**," he hissed through the air.

He pushed and shoved and shoved and pushed and slowly, slowly he moved toward the grass.

The rubber duck began to quack happily and all the other toys began to cheer and smile.

"**RIZZZZZ RIZZZZZ RIZZZZZ**," went the whispering green electric mower. "I believe in myself. I believe in myself. I believe in myself."

Rumble, rumble. Sputter, sputter. Whirring and humming, the green electric mower made his way through the tall grass, until at last he reached the middle of the yard where the cheerfully dotted bouncy ball was stuck.

"Hurray, hurray," cried the yellow rubber duck and all the other toys.

Beaming, the cheerfully dotted bouncy ball rolled out of the grass, happily bounced around and looked up. "Because of you, I am no longer stuck in this thick and tall grass! Thank you for helping me, whispering green electric mower."

And the green electric mower smiled and said with renewed confidence, "I knew I could. I knew I could. I knew I could."

The End

ABOUT THE AUTHOR

Yvonne Jones was born in former East Germany to a German mother and a Vietnamese father. Thus, she spent an inordinate amount of her youth nosing through books that she shouldn't have been reading, and watching movies that she shouldn't have been watching. It was a good childhood.

Always drawing inspiration from her own two children, she loves to write about unique interests and aspires to find fun and exciting ways to have kids discover and learn about the magnificent marvels this world has to offer.

She can be found online at **www.Yvonne-Jones.com**.

A WORD BY THE AUTHOR

If you enjoyed this book, it would be wonderful if you could take a short minute to leave a lovely review on Amazon, as your kind feedback is very appreciated and so very important. It gives me, the author, encouragement for bad days when I want to take up scorpion petting. Thank you so very much for your time!

MORE WORKS BY THIS AUTHOR

The Case of the Mona Lisa – The Amulet of Amser Series (1)
The Case of the Starry Night – The Amulet of Amser Series (2)
The Case of Venus de Milo – The Amulet of Amser Series (3)
The Impatient Little Vacuum
A Gemstone Adventure – Prince Gem of Ology's Royal Quest
Safety Goose: Children's Safety – One Rhyme at a Time ***
Growing Up in East Germany – My Childhood Series (1)
Teeny Totty Uses Mama's Big Potty: Transition from Potty Chair to Toilet
Got Garbage? The Garbage Book for the Biggest Garbage Fan

*** Visit **www.Yvonne-Jones.com** to receive a FREE eBook version of this book

66844263R00024

Made in the USA
Middletown, DE
07 September 2019